SHOP DEAD

SHOP DEAD

Kate Cann

WORLD BOOK DAY
£1

■▯SCHOLASTIC

Scholastic Children's Books
Commonwealth House, 1–19 New Oxford Street,
London, WC1A 1NU, UK
a division of Scholastic Ltd
London ~ New York ~ Toronto ~ Sydney ~ Auckland
Mexico City ~ New Delhi ~ Hong Kong

First published in the UK by Scholastic Ltd, 2001

ISBN 0 439 99346 6

Typeset by TW Typesetting, Midsomer Norton, Somerset
Printed by Cox & Wyman Ltd, Reading, Berks

10 9 8 7 6 5 4 3 2 1

Maybe if I'd had a sister, it would have been different. Maybe – if I'd had a sister – it would have been all right.

Girls have always knocked me out. I don't just mean the normal way girls knock you out and make you want to get your hands on them – although I feel that way, too. What I mean is – girls intrigue me. Completely. I like watching them, the way they move, the way they talk together, the way they do their nails and stuff, all the time they spend on their clothes and their hair. All the stuff other guys get fed up with.

It's like – I dunno – girls aren't just *there*, like guys are, or, you know, horses are or something. The really gorgeous ones have to make themselves up – put themselves together. It's – *creative*. That's what intrigues me.

Maybe though, as I say, if I'd had a sister, I'd have had a gutful of it all – never getting in the bathroom, watching all that clothes havoc before she went off to a club, hearing the drama if her hair went wrong. Maybe I wouldn't think it was creative, then. Maybe I'd think it was a pain in the arse.

And maybe, then, I'd never have fallen for Melanie.

I saw her in my second week at college. I'd been wandering round ever since I got there with my tongue hanging out. All these new girls everywhere, girls I'd never seen before, all in their new gear for the start of term, no more school uniform – it was too much. I don't know how I made it to the right places to register and listen to lectures and eat, I really don't. I was in this kind of daze, just watching them all. And some of them were watching me, too, because I'm not that bad-looking if you want to know the truth. I'm kind of big, too. I look like I've grown up.

Anyway. There I was, wandering, and looking, all kind of luxurious and which-one-shall-I-go-for, when I saw Melanie. I found out later she was called Melanie. Strutting up the steps to the library, great shape, bit too thin maybe, long, long legs, with all this chestnutty hair pulled over to one side and this neat, rusty-coloured skirt and black jacket – and that was it. I was poleaxed. I staggered like an alcoholic up the steps after her and went into the library and flashed my card and pulled any old book off the shelves. Then I saw her go into one of the alcoves and sit down and I followed her in and sat down right opposite her.

And I got a good look at her face.

Dangerous.

I don't know what it's like for girls when you get near someone you really fancy, but for blokes it's bad news. There's all this pumping going round your body, everything screaming sex! sex! sex! and you feel about as obvious and lit-up as the dodgems. You'd expect the girl you're homing in on to jump up and start screaming or whacking you with something, but they never do. Maybe they don't realize what's going on or maybe they're just too polite to say. Or maybe they just sit there quietly enjoying what they've done to you.

Anyway. I opened my book, which had to be about quilt-making, didn't it, and I sat there and pretended to read it, and looked at that amazing face. I went from her eyelids down to her nose and stayed a long time on her mouth – then I went all round her neck and into her hair, and back to her eyelids again. That journey didn't help the pounding inside me. I could have done it for ever.

She was flicking through this big black book and jotting notes down in a little spiral-bound notepad. It looked like she might be working, which was not something I could understand, the state I was in right then. After a while, she pulled her bag towards her and rummaged inside and pulled out a little purple case thing and snapped it open and looked into it. It was a mirror – you could tell, just the way she was looking into it. And then this is what killed me. She didn't do anything, just looked. Most girls would get their lippy out or flick at their hair or scrape some mark off their face or something, but not her. She just looked, and smiled, as though there was no improvement she could make.

And she was right, there wasn't. Not one thing.

Then she snapped the case shut, and put it in her bag, followed it with the book and the notepad, and then she looked up at me. She had stunning eyes, violet-coloured and clear like water. She looked into me like I was a mirror too, then she stood up and walked away.

Leaving me totally wiped out. Gone.

The thing is, I'm not completely lacking in confidence around girls, not like some blokes are. I don't want to start bragging and telling you how long my track record is, but I've had a bit of experience. And that's taught me never to hunt in packs, like some blokes do. If you want a night full of loud chat and lots of beer and throwing up and absolutely no contact with the opposite sex, go round in a group of guys. But if you're really after a girl — especially one special girl, like I was — you do it on your own.

It took me three weeks to pull Melanie. I found out about her, and I followed her, and I made eye contact with her, and I stood next to her one sacred day in the canteen queue and exchanged a few comments on the crap food they had on offer. Then I got chatting to some of the people she hung around with and made sure I got asked to the house party she was going to on Friday night.

And then I moved in.

Just the normal stuff. I got her a drink, and I tried to talk to her until the room got too loud for talking, then there was a bit of drunken dancing going on, and we joined in. God, she was perfect. She moved like nothing could touch her, nothing could affect her, like she was on another plane. Then after a bit we went into the kitchen to get another drink and when we left it and walked into the dark corridor, that's when I really moved in.

That's the real test, isn't it. That's when you find out if you're on or not. Well, I was on. And I was so blown away by the fact that she was letting me wrap my arms round her body and put my mouth on her face I suppose I didn't notice much that she wasn't – you know. Responding.

Well, OK. Things had only just started. There was plenty of time.

It was late and the party was coming to a bit of an abrupt finish. You know, parents arrive back, lights-switched-on, "I told you no later than two am and what the *hell's* that on the living room carpet?" So I grabbed her by the hand and towed her outside, and told her I wanted to see her again. Tomorrow.

"Tomorrow's Saturday," she said. "I'm going shopping."

I'd meant tomorrow night, of course, but

I said, "Great. Let me come," expecting her to laugh and say get lost.

But she didn't. She looked up at me, coolly, and said, "OK. I need a new dress. You can tell me what I look like in it."

Woah. I'd never had a girl who'd wanted me to go shopping with her before, and I'd always rather fancied it. Hanging round the mirrors and the changing rooms, trying to look blokeish and bored, watching Melanie fixated on making herself look even more gorgeous … what a turn on.

Shopping? I was on all right.

I met Melanie at eleven o'clock outside Marks and Spencer and she let me kiss her hello on the side of her face about a mile away from her mouth. Then she said, "Ever been to Harum?"

"What?" I said.

"It's a shop. A completely brilliant shop. It's like Biba – you heard of Biba?"

I frowned. I sort of had. "Some old hippy shop, wasn't it? My mum—"

"It wasn't just a shop. It was like a club, a

special place. Somewhere you worked your life out in. Harum's the same. You go in there, you're – different. It's just – it's brilliant. I'll show you." And she turned on her heel and walked off, me following.

It was the longest speech I'd heard her make so far. I caught her up, and got hold of her hand.

She was right, it was a good shop. It made the other fashion shops look tame, formulaic. The minute you walked in there was this strange, purplish light cocooning you from above, with bright, white light beams searching out the racks of clothes. There were all these colours and feathers and silky things and sparkles everywhere, really female. To the left of the door there was a long, low, black sofa that made me want to grab Melanie and stretch out on it. The music was something I didn't know, like New Age stuff with a sting in its tail, and there was this sharp, exciting smell being pumped into the air from somewhere.

"See?" breathed Melanie, like someone

on the threshold of a temple. "Isn't it *fabulous*?"

Then she was off among the racks of clothes, a beagle on the scent, and I followed. The shop seemed to go back and back, two whole floors of it, joined by curving staircases with little lightbulbs like a catwalk. Whoever designed it had style, I can tell you that. There were lots of levels and platforms and spaces, with the racks and shelves making up different shapes in each. And everywhere you looked there were these classy dummies, with long, long legs and blind, beautiful faces, images of what the shoppers could be, maybe, if they'd buy the same clothes.

I followed Melanie up and down and in and out, my eyes never leaving her. I watched as she held tops and skirts and dresses up against herself in front of a mirror, then in front of me, and got a hundred per cent positive response from both. I stood behind her as she flicked through racks of shirts and rows of nail varnish, and I breathed it all in like perfume.

She was – I don't know – *shining*. It was like she'd really come alive, in that shop. She didn't take any notice of me, but I was allowed to be there, to follow her, to watch her. She was my passport to this world, and she was queen in it, too. It just about blew me away.

After a long, long time Melanie selected a couple of dresses off two different racks and headed over to where a white neon sign flashed *Changing Room* in huge, jagged letters. She disappeared through the curtains and I waited outside until she reappeared, like a conjuror's assistant, and pirouetted for me.

"Brilliant," I croaked, soon as I could speak. "Knock out."

"I'm not sure. Hang on and I'll show you the other one."

Soon she was there again in front of me, in a different dress, twizzling round, looking fabulous. "I don't know, Mel," I said.

"Melanie," she said.

"Sorry. I don't know. They're both –

they're *stunning*. You look as good as one of those dummies."

As soon as that was out of my mouth I regretted it, because it didn't sound exactly flattering, but Melanie glowed as though I'd paid her the best compliment in the world.

"Come on – which dress?" she smiled.

"I like the front on that one," I said. I did, too. It was the lowest.

"Yeah. But this *colour* – I think the other's better on me."

"Get both."

"I can't afford *both*. I can't really afford *one*. But I'm going to get the other one. I think. I'll just try it on one more time."

Fifteen more minutes of waiting and complimenting, and I was trailing Melanie to the cash point, where this icily-perfect woman took her credit card and put the dress into a slick little carrier with real rope handles. As soon as she'd got the bag in her hands, Melanie acted like someone who'd had a shot of something exciting. She practically danced through the shop in front of me, then she announced, "I want to get my face made over."

"What?"

"A makeover. I want to try that new tawny look."

Now I've seen women undergoing make-up counter humiliation before – they get perched on a stool while some sneering sadist with rigid hair splats on foundation and tells them their eye-shadow's all wrong. "You sure you want to?" I asked, but she'd already headed off.

The make-up section was serious stuff. It was screened off, sort of scientific-Japanese, and they had these reclining chairs, like dentists' chairs, that they got you to lie on while they did you over. They welcomed Melanie almost wordlessly, as though there was no need to discuss what needed to be done. I watched as they cleaned off her perfect face and resurrected it again, all glowing with clever sparkly gold bits on the eyes.

I was beginning to run out of compliments by this time, but Melanie hardly noticed. She pranced off, and stopped in front of this little stage thing where three dummies were arranged in unlikely but kind of erotic positions. Then she said, "Spot the difference," stepped up beside them and posed alongside.

OK, she wasn't quite as thin and long as them, no human could be, but she blended in all right. She held her position so still. There was some kind of smoke machine at the back sending out this vague blue mist, and it wrapped round all four of them, and they looked so lovely, so lifeless… It gave me the creeps a bit, if you want to know the truth.

I called out that we should go and get a drink, and something to eat, and there was a long pause, then she stepped forward and got down off the little stage. Then we went to a café, and while I was eating and she was playing with a cappuccino, she announced she was feeling tired, she wanted to go home.

"What about tonight?" I said. "We could go to that new club on the high street."

She looked dubious and I added, "You could try out your new dress…"

We met at ten-thirty, and she was wearing her new dress, and she still had on the make-up they'd done for her, and she looked amazing.

It was a good night, except – except I should have been happier than I was, being in a new club with my arm wrapped round someone who looked as good as she did. She just wasn't shining, like she had done in the shop. She seemed – drained, somehow, tired, and I wasn't getting through to her. She hardly ever looked at me and she only half-listened to the stuff I tried to talk about.

I began to wonder if she even liked me. I began to wonder why she'd agreed to go out with me in the first place.

We did some dancing, and then we stopped and I got her sort of pinned up against one of the mirrored walls. "So how come you said yes to me, Melanie?" I asked.

"Said yes?" she repeated.

"Said you'd come out with me?"

In answer she laid both hands flat on my chest, and lifted her face up to mine. You don't carry on talking when a girl does that. At the end of the second long kiss, I opened my eyes and saw that hers were wide, staring behind her.

Looking at our reflections in the mirrored wall.

So it was set. Our relationship, I mean – what passed for our relationship. We didn't spend much time together at college because we were doing completely different courses, and because Melanie never seemed to want lunch. But we'd meet in the evening sometimes, and we'd spend every Saturday together.

Shopping.

"You're barking, mate," said my friend, Max. "Every week?"

"Yep."

"All day?"

"Just about."

"You in love with her or something?"

"No," I said, and I realized I wasn't. "It's just – you've seen her."

"Yeah," he replied. "She's a knockout. But come on. All that girly stuff – every Saturday?"

Max had three sisters. He wouldn't understand if I told him what a buzz it gave me, watching Melanie put herself together. He wouldn't understand if I told him I got totally turned on looking at Melanie look at clothes in shops.

And if that sounds sad, too bad – it's true. Shops were where she was most exciting, and she was always wilder after she'd bought something. I'm not going to spell it out, but it was like she wouldn't stop me doing anything.

But of course there's only so much you can do on a bench in a shopping precinct.

After maybe six weeks of shopping every Saturday, I suggested to Melanie we went somewhere else. Just for a change. Swimming. Bowling. Or take my motorbike out to somewhere rural and get lunch in a pub. She looked at me as though I'd lost it. "Maybe next week," she said. "I need to get shoes this week."

Next week never arrived, of course. There was always some article of clothing she *needed*. And I began to get – bored isn't the right word. I was uneasy. What had been a thrill was becoming a chill. I still liked to watch her, but it made me feel – I don't know. Like I was watching someone in the throes of addiction.

I still hadn't got through to her, either. We had almost no good conversation together, and we never had a laugh. And she'd cry off in the evening time after time, say she was exhausted. I had these thoughts about dumping her, but then I'd look at her, and I'd see the jealous faces of other guys as we walked along the road together, hand in hand, and I'd think – *not yet. Give it a bit longer.*

Then something happened in my English class. We were reading some Edgar Allen Poe, the nineteenth-century master of horror. Florid, swallowed-the-dictionary stuff, but pretty gripping, too. One story particularly got to me. It was about an artist who was painting a portrait of his new wife up in a turret somewhere, making her sit for hours and hours. She drooped and faded, but he was too much of a sod to notice. All the time, the portrait was getting better and better, more life-like, and the girl was getting more ill. Then he finishes it, and he's really pleased with it. "This is indeed Life itself!" he says. Then he turns to his wife, and – you've guessed it – she's dead.

I didn't know at first why that story made me think of Melanie, but it did, and I couldn't get it out of my mind. And then I worked out the connection when I was home alone a couple of nights later after quite a few beers.

Melanie was the painting, and the wife. She was *both*. All her make-up, the clothes, the show – that was like the portrait. And all the other sides to Melanie were just – *dying*. If they'd been there in the first place.

I sat there and thought, and made up my mind I had to dump her.

Soon.

Then that Saturday something amazing happened, something that turned my decision on its head. We met as usual outside Marks and Spencers and she said, "All I need to get today is a new top. I thought purple, to go with those white trousers I got last week. And then – d'you fancy coming round to my house? Only I've got the place to myself." And she fixed me with a slightly scary violet stare.

"Sure," I said, while everything inside me started pumping up fit to explode. "Great."

All my thoughts about dumping her fled. I told her I'd see her in Harum, because I wanted to drop into Smith's and pick up the new *SuperBikes*, and then I went straight into Boots instead and got myself equipped.

She must mean it, I said to myself, she must *really* mean it – otherwise why make the point that she'd got the house to herself? I had this little niggly goody-goody thought that it wasn't exactly showing character to sleep with a girl the exact same week you'd decided to dump her, but I trod it underfoot.

Maybe this is what we *need* for our relationship, I told myself. Maybe Melanie's the sort who just finds conversation hard, who finds connecting with people hard. She must really like me, after all, or she wouldn't have asked me back, would she, and made such a big thing about having the house to herself. Maybe this'll be the turning point.

And then I stopped any more analysing – if I'm honest, any more *thinking*. Apart from thoughts that involved Melanie letting me take off all her carefully-chosen designer clothes one after the other and chuck them on the bed.

Her house was really normal. I don't quite know what I was expecting – something like the cover of *House Beautiful*, maybe, all jugs of white lilies and fat white sofas. But it wasn't. It was ordinary, and tidy, and a bit chintzy, and the only really squirmy thing was all the photos of Melanie everywhere. Most homes have a few photos – I myself had just threatened my folks with violence if they didn't remove a particularly nasty one of me with too much hair and no teeth – but this was seriously over the top. Lining the hall, in the kitchen, on top of the telly – everywhere.

"Want to see my room?" Melanie said. That was more like it. I climbed up the stairs behind her, and she walked to the end of the landing (past about a hundred more photos of her face) and pushed open a door. "After you," she said. I walked in – and jumped backwards like a rat from a trap, crashing into Melanie. I nearly passed out in fright, I swear. There was this *girl*, behind the door, kind of reaching out towards me, and staring –

"Idiot," smirked Melanie. "That's Tandy. And she can't hurt you."

It was only one of the stupid dummies from Harum, wasn't it. I laughed out loud, but I felt really spooked. My heart was thumping and my mouth had gone all dry. I tried to turn it into a big joke – I got hold of its hard, plastic hand, and shook it, and said, "Hi, Tandy. Thanks for scaring the life out of me."

"Give her a kiss, too," giggled Melanie.

Oh God, I thought, but I craned up and landed a smacker on its nasty cold mouth. "How d'you get hold of it, Melanie?" I asked. "Her, I mean."

"They have a big bin, behind Harum, and they chuck bits of the dummies out sometimes. A leg, or an arm – I got her head and her torso at the same time, and the rest I just kind of collected. And put her together."

Gruesome, I thought. "Great," I muttered.

"I've got other bits, too. Look." And she pointed over to some shelves at the far side of her room, and there, lined up like some waxworks horror film, were three hands, two arms, and a disembodied head.

The head was particularly disturbing.

"That's Kathy," Melanie said, fondly.

"She's my make-up double. I try out faces on her, and then I use them on myself."

This was getting creepier by the minute. The hands all had different colour nail varnishes on. "You try stuff out on them, too?" I asked.

Melanie shrugged. "Sometimes."

"So … *Tandy* … she's like your big … Barbie?" I went on. "Life in plastic – it's fantastic?"

"I try out my outfits on her," she said, coldly. "Colour combinations, stuff like that."

"Why don't you just try them out on yourself?"

Melanie didn't answer. She turned her back to me, and walked into the middle of her room. Clothes covered every surface; hanging from the picture rail, piled on the chair. Shop carrier-bags crammed with new gear were stacked against the walls. The wardrobe door was open, overflowing with dresses. Melanie pulled a feather boa from a hook, went over to Tandy, wrapped it round her neck, and started crooning to her. "You're beautiful," she was murmuring. "Don't listen to him. You're *beautiful*."

As the start to a seduction scene, this was not going well. I felt *in the way*, like I was intruding on the two of them. And her over-stuffed room gave me the heebies. I felt about as turned on as a cold kipper. Just the thought of trying to make out with those two dead, perfect dummy faces watching me was too much.

Pull yourself together, I nagged myself. How often does a girl ask you up to her room? "Come on, Melanie," I said. "We haven't come here to play dollies." And I got hold of her, all kind of he-man, and pulled her on to the bed with me, and started kissing her.

But I stayed like a cold kipper. Every time I shut my eyes I'd think of that weird dummy, and the way it stared, and kind of clawed its hands out towards me, and every time I opened my eyes I'd – well, I'd see it, wouldn't I. And the severed head as well. So I'd shut my eyes again and land my mouth on Melanie's and I felt like…

I felt like I was kissing the dummy.

Talk about an anti-aphrodisiac. I got as far as undoing the top two buttons on Melanie's shirt and then it was like I flipped. I jumped up, made some muttered excuse about a migraine kicking in, and legged it down the stairs at the speed of light. "I'll see you, Melanie," I called back, at the front door. "I'll phone."

I didn't though. Not all week. Instead, I thought about how I was going to finish with her that Saturday, what I was going to say. And then Friday night I got a phone call. It was Melanie, warmer than I'd ever heard her before. "I missed you, baby!" she cooed. "Where've you been?"

"Um, you know," I said. "Work and stuff."

"You know what you said about going out to the country, on your motorbike?" she went on. "Well, why don't we, tomorrow? It's s'posed to be really sunny."

"Um, well, I – well I…"

"Yes?" said Melanie.

"OK. I'll pick you up. Twelve o'clock?"

Mr Make-a-Decision-and-Act-on-It, that's me. Mr Firm-Resolve. I told myself I wasn't really backing down. I told myself I could just as soon finish with her on a day trip to the country as outside Marks and Spencer, where we usually met. It was rubbish, of course. Now all my mental practising was out of sync. When I rehearsed my "we're through" speech in my head, I saw shops. How could I dump her in the country, near a load of trees?

And anyway – she was trying harder, now. Maybe she'd realized I was going to dump her, and she was doing what she needed to stop that happening, but she was definitely bringing more to the relationship. She was the one who'd *suggested* going to the country. This was a new development. Maybe she did have other sides to her. Maybe I'd got it wrong.

Whatever. She looked fantastic when I drove round to collect her – so fantastic that I forgot that nasty session in her bedroom. She'd put her hair up, so you could see even more of that amazing face, and she had this wonderful silky-looking sleeveless top on.

"You should put something over that," I said, reluctantly.

"I won't be cold," she answered. "I'll be up close to you."

Woah.

"It's more for protection…" I began, then I tailed off. She looked gorgeous. I handed her my spare helmet, and tried to do it up for her, but she pushed me off because she said I was screwing up her hair. Then we went outside and she put her hands on my shoulders as she climbed up behind me on the bike.

Talk about being split in two – I was in an agony of indecision. As we headed out of town my mind was making up one list of why I should dump her and another list of why I shouldn't, and trying to compare the two – and maybe that's why I didn't react as quickly as I could have done when that great van turned out of a slip-road too quickly and careered across the lanes into us and sent us skidding.

★ ★ ★

"Absolutely not your fault, son," said the copper. "Nothing you could've done."

That's kind of comforting to hear when your leg's twisted back at a nasty angle and your shoulder's killing you and you feel like half the skin's come off your arms and you can't see straight without stars. Someone was pushing a needle into my arm.

"What about Melanie?" I groaned. "Is she – is she – ?"

"She'll be fine. Her face is a bit cut up and she's lost some blood, but she'll be fine."

Her face is a bit cut up. I thought of Melanie's perfect skin and I could feel myself breaking into a sweat.

"*Why* is she – *Where* is she – ?"

"Well, her helmet came off as she skidded. Looks like the strap wasn't done up properly."

Oh God, oh no! "That was *my fault*," I wailed. "I should've checked it, it's old but it's *fine* if you—"

"Hey, hey, calm down, son. It did the job

it was supposed to do – it kept her alive. Now let's get you in the ambulance."

I wanted to ask him how badly she was hurt, how much of her face, but whatever they'd given me took over and I was out.

They told me I'd only be in hospital for about a week. My leg was damaged the worst – I'd need physio for a while and maybe an op on the knee later, they said, but it wasn't like I'd never walk again or anything. Everyone kept telling me how lucky I'd been, which I couldn't get my head round – why is it lucky to be mown down by some casual madman who shouldn't have been in charge of a trike, let alone a van? Still, I suppose they meant it could have been a lot worse.

Which it could have been. It was for Melanie.

They stitched up her face and neck as best they could, but you could tell there'd be some serious scarring. It was all down one side, the side that had skidded along the ground.

When they tried telling her she was lucky, lucky her helmet had protected her skull on impact, she'd just stare at them blankly. Superficial wounding, they called it, but for her, it was deep as it could go.

I gave up all thoughts of dumping her, of course. I couldn't have been that cruel. And as soon as they let me up and about with crutches I hobbled down to her ward to see her.

I found her bed at the end of the ward, with the curtains half-closed about it. A youngish-looking nurse came round from the other side of the bed and said, a bit starchily, "Hi. You must be the owner of the bike."

"Yeah," I said, defensively.

"You look like you got off lighter than she did."

"I did. And look – don't try to make me feel worse about this than I do already, 'cos that's impossible, OK?"

She smiled at me then, and her face softened. "I'm not trying to make you feel worse," she said. "I heard it wasn't your fault."

In the bed, Melanie hadn't moved. Half her face and all down one arm was covered by white gauze and plasters. "How is she?" I muttered.

"Why don't you ask her?" said the nurse. "You're supposed to be her boyfriend, aren't you?"

I moved round the bed, and nervously put my hand over one of hers. Bandages came almost to the tips of her fingers. "Melanie?" I whispered. "It's me."

Her eye, the one eye I could see, flicked open, registered me, and closed again.

"Melanie? Are you OK?"

The nurse gave a sort of sigh, then she moved away, saying, "I'll leave you to it."

I really wanted to ask her to stay, but I didn't. "Melanie," I said again. "Melanie."

Melanie opened her eye again and fixed it on me. Then her mouth opened. You could see nearly all of that, beside the bandages. "Why?" she croaked. "*Why?*"

"I *know*," I said, desperately, "I know. It's

the pits, it's — I can't tell you. I'm so sorry. I'm so sorry, Mel. Melanie."

There was a long silence, and her eye closed again and tears welled out from behind her eyelid. I began to feel I couldn't bear it, like I had to call for a nurse or something. "They told me about you," I said urgently, desperate to comfort. "It's not that bad, really it's not. They said the worst was your neck and they might try skin grafts and you can wear high collars and stuff, can't you, Melanie…" I drivelled to a halt, and looked wildly about the ward, but there was no one there, no one. "It won't look that bad," I repeated, helplessly.

Her violet eye opened again, and looked at me with such blank hatred I thought I might pass out. "Go away," she hissed.

I stumbled to my feet and swung out of the ward with my crutches going as fast as I could. In the corridor outside, the nurse called out, "How d'you get on?"

"She won't speak to me," I said. "She told me to go away."

The nurse shrugged. "Can't blame her, I guess."

"No. No, I s'pose not. But she looked at me like she wanted me to die."

"Well, as I say, you can't blame her," the nurse repeated, depressingly, adding: "You might have stayed with her a bit longer." Then she shrugged, dismissing me, and I remembered the way Melanie's one eye had closed and I suddenly felt terrible – lonely, scared, awful.

"I couldn't," I muttered, desperately. "I mean – I – I *couldn't*."

"But you're her boyfriend."

"I don't feel like her boyfriend. We just didn't *connect*. We had nothing to talk about. And I – it's – it's really sick. I was going to finish with her. The day we had the accident."

The nurse folded her arms and looked at me, really hard. "And will you now?"

"What – finish with her? *No*. Of course not. Look – I feel *awful* about this. It was my fault, it was my bike. And I should have made her wear my jacket – I should have *made* her let me do the helmet up properly. I feel so guilty I – I just wish it could have been me not her, I'd give *anything* –"

"Why wouldn't she let you do up the helmet?"

"She pushed me off – she said I was messing up her hair."

"Oh, good grief. Look, it's not that bad. Especially not on the face. It'll heal, over time. Stop beating yourself up."

"I can't help it."

"No, I know. Look, love, I can't stand here chatting. Go and get yourself a cup of coffee or something."

"OK," I muttered. "Look – I'll come back in the morning, OK?"

She nodded, and smiled, and I felt a tiny bit better as I heaved my way down to the canteen.

The next day, I hobbled along to the women's ward to visit Melanie once more. She'd been moved to the centre of the ward, probably in an attempt to cheer her up, but she looked more isolated than ever.

All the other beds had at least one visitor beside them; she had none. One bunch of sad-looking flowers that should have been ditched days ago drooped in a vase by the head.

"Melanie?" I called, gently. "Melanie?"

She opened her one free eye and looked. "Why are you here?"

"Well, I—"

"I don't want to see you."

"Melanie – look. You'll come through this. I'll help you, I'll—"

"*Leave me alone.*"

It was so venomous, so absolute, I turned away immediately. The nurse from yesterday appeared at my side and smiled at me, consolingly. "She's bound to be a bit tense," she said. "Her bandages come off tomorrow."

"Oh, God. Cover all the mirrors."

"That's not a nice thing to say."

"No. Sorry. It's just—"

"It's only a few scars, you know. You're going to have to tell her it's what's inside that counts, not what's outside."

I looked at the nurse hopelessly, couldn't think of a thing to say.

"You boys are all the same," she said impatiently. "No wonder young girls are so hung up on their appearance. And that one – she needs support, now. She's had no one to visit her, only you. We can't get in touch with her mother. You know her family?"

I shook my head.

"Something weird going on there," she went on. "We're really worried about her." Then she paused, looking straight at me. "D'you know someone called Tandy?"

I felt my stomach lurch; my face freeze over into vacancy. I shook my head.

"Or Kathy? Know a Kathy? They must be friends of hers, I reckon. In her sleep, she's crying for them. Calling out for them."

I hobbled away.

Back in my ward, I found my doctor waiting impatiently. "Ah – the wanderer returns!" he boomed. "Obviously no need to keep you in here any longer. Let me see you walk without those crutches." And he just about snatched them away from me. I felt like falling over, just to show him, but I didn't. I took three awkward steps along the lino instead.

"Excellent!" he pronounced. "You can go first thing tomorrow, lad. We need your bed."

Terrific. Actually, it *was* terrific. I was desperate to get out. Desperate to sleep in real darkness and silence once more. Desperate to – desperate to get away.

The next day I collected a sheaf of stuff about outpatients' visits and exercises, then Mum arrived at nine sharp to collect me. She asked me if I wanted to say goodbye to Melanie, and I said no, better not. Then, later, she offered to drive me back for the evening visit, but I said maybe tomorrow.

I told myself Melanie wouldn't want to see anyone right away, not once her bandages had come off. I told myself I was letting her get used to it first.

The fact is, I was scared. I felt really, really sorry for her – but I was scared of her more. Scared of what was going on inside her. I left it for two whole days before I phoned the hospital, got through to her ward at the start of the evening shift. "She discharged herself," said the sister, tartly. "Unofficially."

"You mean she—"

"Walked out. Yes. Two hours ago, in fact. Medically, she was fine to go. We're a bit concerned with how she's coping with the disfigurement, though. And we still haven't got in touch with her family. I think a health visitor's going to call … going to try to, anyway. We see worse cases all the time, frankly."

I rang off. Then I headed upstairs and threw myself down on the bed. With everything in me I wished I'd never got involved with Melanie. I just wanted to turn away, forget about her. I knew I should go to her house, but I couldn't face it. I remembered her creepy bedroom, and the dummies, and all the photos every-where. And who was her mum – what kind of mum doesn't visit her daughter in hospital? I sat there, all hunched up and screwed up, and this old memory filtered into my head. It was when I'd still been trailing Melanie, trying to get her to notice me. I'd sat at the next table along from her and her mates, and I'd listened to their chat, all about this girl they knew who had this really big birthmark on her face. They were saying how well she coped with it — how she covered it up with make-up, although it couldn't hide it completely, and just got *on* with things. Most of the girls there were saying how they admired her; wondering whether they'd cope as well. And then Melanie said she couldn't stand it, being like that.

Melanie said she'd rather be dead.

I had to see her. I had to see she was all right. I got off my bed, went down to the garage and got my motorbike out. Dad had come over all "get the boy back in the saddle" and had it fixed for me. I felt pretty nervous, wheeling it out of the garage, because it was the first time I'd got it out since the crash, but I was driven on by this weird sense of urgency. I climbed on and revved it, and legged it on to the road. Then I forgot about being nervous about riding it. Panic was filling me; I accelerated fast. I could feel my damaged knee aching, protesting, but I ignored it.

I screeched to a halt outside Melanie's house, ran up her front path, and banged on the door. No answer. The house was in darkness. I banged again, louder. Nothing. Somehow, I knew there'd be nothing. I turned, headed back to the road, and as I swung the bike round its headlight shone on something lying in the gutter.

It was a hand, a dummy hand. Three red nails, two purple ones. The sight of it flooded me with inexplicable fear. It meant something – I knew it meant something – something bad. I got on the bike and accelerated off.

I was on the outskirts of town when I heard the sirens. A pack of them, police cars and fire engines, screaming like furies, heading into the centre where the shops were. The noise filled my head like

terror. I slammed on the brakes in the
middle of the road, checked my mirrors,
and wrenched the bike round in a U-turn.
Then I floored the accelerator, following
the sirens into town.

I knew, somehow I knew, exactly where
they were headed.

When I reached the precinct I turned
the engine off and legged the bike the last
few metres. Then I stopped. Harum was
going up in flames, huge bright flames,
yellow and red against the night sky.
Firemen were breaking windows with axes
and battling into the shop, hoses on at full
force. People were running from all direc-
tions towards the blaze; two policemen
were trying to hold them back.

Melanie's shop. She knew that shop
better than anyone. She'd know where its
weak points were. She'd know where to
break in.

And then a fireman ran from the shop,
mouth gaping in horror. "There's a *pile*," he
croaked, "*bodies* —"

I left the bike and started to run. I

pushed past the fireman, through the smashed door of the shop. The ground-floor flames had been doused; thick smoke swirled, making my eyes stream. In the centre of the store was a pile of legs and arms and heads, like the clear-up after a massacre, smoking, smouldering. My legs had collapsed in shock at the same time as my brain was telling me it was OK, it was OK, I knew what they were.

I walked towards the pile. As the smoke cleared, you could see it wasn't human. Dummies. Beautiful dummies. Legs, faces, hair, arms, melting, curling, blackened, ruined. I saw Tandy, just before her face fell in. And one arm, right at the top, that wasn't melting. It was burning, like meat burns on a barbecue, like flesh burns.

You're not like them now, Melanie, I thought, stupidly.

You're a lot less like them dead than alive.

If you liked

SHOP DEAD

you'll love

HARD CASH

the first book in Kate Cann's brilliant series from Scholastic. Try it now, and you'll be rushing out to the bookshop…

My name's Rich. Which is funny, because at this moment I have only 72p in the pocket of my worn out jacket and no prospect of getting my hands on any more until Friday. I can't afford clothes. I can't afford booze. I can't afford anything. Every single one of my art pencils needs replacing and I can't afford that, either. I daren't even sharpen the bloody things when I need to now. If they get much shorter I'll be holding them with tweezers.

Money. It does your head in. Not having it, I mean.

I saw this bloke on the way home tonight. He was one-handedly trying to park his brand-new BMW convertible in a very narrow space and all the time he was jerking back and forth he was jabbering into this flashy little silver mobile. I stood there, in the shadow of the tree by my gate, and stared at him, and my stomach went into this tight hot knot of hate and envy.

He jammed the car to a stop, not straight, as though it wouldn't really matter if someone took his sidelight off because he could always get another sidelight – or another car – and jumped out. Everything about him gave off money vibrations. His suit, his shoes, the way his hair was cut, the way his body and face were a little bit plump but still shining and toned, like he ate and drank very well but then worked it off at some high-tech gym afterwards.

He went round to the boot of the car and hauled out a classy-looking sports bag, two carriers from one of those late-night top-price delis, and a bunch of lilies. Then he slammed the boot shut, locked it with a noisy remote, and headed off across the street.

I stared after him, and I wanted to kill him. You sleek bastard. You're going to leg it into your smart flat and whip up whatever designer-foody goodies you have stashed in that bag and then some top bird is going to come round and you'll pop some champagne and give her the lilies and she'll end up shagging you with all her silky clothes chucked around the place. And the real pain of it is this is just normal workaday stuff for you. This is life.

And I can't even afford a couple of sodding pencils.

To the rich shall be given more – all the food all the cars all the booze all the birds yeah even until the ending of the earth.

And the poor had just better get over it.

"Be grateful you've got a roof over your head and food on the table," Mum always says. With a look that implies that I'm an ungrateful git. Which I probably am. I walk up our path and let myself into our skinny little hall that's needed redecorating for five years and more. Every spring, Dad makes some joke like, "Why don't you do it, Richard? You're supposed to be able to paint." And I think maybe I should, but I don't ever get round to it.

"Mum?"

"In here, luv. In the kitchen."

"What's for supper?"

"Spag bol."

"Great, Mum. I'm starved."

"When aren't you? Grate me up that cheese, luv."

We don't have proper Parmesan on our spag bol. We have old Cheddar that Mum gets cheap from the market. It's OK – smells as bad. She does OK with the pathetically small amount she has to spend on food each week.

They're proud of how well they budget, my parents. To hear them talk, you'd think budgeting was every bit as good as having money.

Dad walks through the door and looks at me in the raised-chin, challenging way he's used ever since I got more or less sanely past puberty. Dad challenges most people, especially men, and Mum says he could've got a lot further in his line of work if he didn't do it quite so much. But he says it's better to be hard up and keep your pride.

Maybe he's right.

"So how was college, son?" he asks.

"Oh, OK. Got bollocked by Huw again."

"Why?"

"Late assignment."

"Good God, d'you ever do an assignment you don't give in late?"

I shrug. "It was a crap topic."

"He's the teacher, son, not you. If he sets you a topic it's because you need it for your grades."

"I don't see what drawing a pile of lemons and crap has to do with anything."

"Nor do I, but if he sets it, you do it, right?"

"Leave him alone, Bill," says Mum tiredly.

"Yeah, leave me alone, Dad," I say. Sometimes I think he just asks me stuff so he can jump on something and lecture me about it. He's on my back the whole time. It does my head in if you want the truth.

"Call Sam for me," Mum says to Dad. "It'll be ready in five minutes." Dad stomps out to the hall to yell up the stairs for my little brother Sam, and Mum says, "Work isn't the only reason you're fed up, is it?"

I shrug.

"You still mooning after that girl?"

I shrug again. I could shrug for England, I reckon.

"I don't know, Rich. Why don't you just ask her out?"

"'Cos she'd say no."

"Course she wouldn't. Good-looking boy like you."

"I can't afford to ask her out."

"Good God, you'd think feminism had never happened. Girls don't expect to get paid for nowadays."

"Girls like Portia McCutcheon do."

Mum dips her mouth in the way that says, "She's not worth it then."

Maybe she isn't, but I'll never get the chance to find out, will I?"

Sam bursts in talking to Dad about football, just like I used to do, and we all sit down and eat and Dad tells me to cheer up and I hate myself for being so miserable and sour. It's not my folks' fault they're not rich. They're great — well, Mum is — loads better than some of the jerks I see letting themselves in and out of the remote-controlled gates of the posh tenements just up our street. It's just—

My parents are the salt of the earth and yes salt glitters but not like diamonds do.

I had a job two months ago. It lasted three weeks. I worked two nights, sometimes three, in this bar in town. It was brilliant. OK pay, free food, free beer — that's what did me in, of course. I liked the beer too much. And I got totally pissed once too often and got fired, with no hope of a reference. Not that there were any other jobs to go for. Bar jobs are like gold dust in this place.

Sam has a paper round. The little sod's a lot richer than I am and what's he got to spend it on? Chewing gum and hair gel, that's all. The odd trip to lie his way into a 15 movie. I've considered asking him for a loan but, Christ, you've got to have some pride.

Last week Dad said I could do the

sweeping up Saturdays at his factory and got very short with me when I turned it down. Pride again. But I mean, *me* – sweeping up?

Anyway, it was OK to turn it down because I've got a plan. Mum still slips me a few quid every Friday, about a fiver, whatever she can afford. And this Friday I'm spending it on stamps. I've already blagged five big A2 envelopes out of the stationery cupboard outside the Art Department. And I've got five sets of six of my top drawings – I managed to photocopy them when the office was empty of all but Charlotte, who thinks I'm a "nice boy" because I don't have excess body-piercing like most of the art lot.

These drawings are – they're good. Even Huw said they're good. "Christ, though, boy," he said. "Look at the pain in these. Look at the barely-repressed rage. We should get you some therapy. Mind you, if these scribbles are indications of your inner being, what therapist would knowingly go anywhere near it?"

Ha, ha. Huw reckons he's a real funny man. My pictures are pretty dark though. Monsters and ghouls and nightmares. But they're *strong*. They come off the page at you, alive – more alive than most stuff in the real world. I love them and I loved doing them. And now I'm sending them out to try to make myself some money.

I've done my research. I've got the names of five little local companies – three advertising, two graphic design. With the help of Charlotte I've written out five really good letters, that stop just this side of actual begging, saying, This is a sample of my work and I'll do anything for you, anything at all.

I can hear you saying I haven't got a hope in hell. I can hear you saying, You'd have better odds if you spent your money on lottery tickets, not stamps.

Yeah, well, maybe you're right, but I've got to try, right? I'm desperate.

I get up late the next day and get into college even later, and miss the lecture on

Impressionism. Well who cares, everyone knows they only painted that way 'cos they needed specs. I ought to go into the art rooms and do some work but instead I edge past them just about flat against the wall in case Huw spots me and bursts out demanding his Lemons Portrait. By this time it's nearly lunchtime and I can't afford lunch but I think, sod it, I'll go and get a cup of tea to stave off the hunger pangs and just as I'm walking through the cafeteria door I bump smack into Portia.

We're visual people, we artists. And Portia is visual dynamite. Today on her stunning body she's wearing a little short jumper that probably cost about and hundred quid and tight classy jeans. And her hair is black and silky and her face is pointed and perfectly symmetrical like a cat's.

She's with her friend Jenny and she's eating a bag of chips. "*Hi*, Richy," she says. She always says the *hi* kind of half seductive, half sarcastic when she talks to me. I know she fancies me – she flirts with me and teases me but then she walks off because I'm scruffy with crap hair I cut myself and I'm always broke. She's a snob. I hate myself for having such a thing about a snob. But I don't have control over my feelings, do I?

"Hi," I say. "Did you get to the lecture?"

"Yes. Didn't you?"

"No. I forgot to get up."

"*Yeah?*" she smirks, with this sexy kind of overlay in her voice. "Tired were you?"

Jenny giggles. Jenny giggles a lot. It's hysteria brought on by the pride of being Portia's best mate, I reckon.

"Just asleep," I say.

"Well you didn't miss much. They gave out these sheets. Want to photocopy them?" And she waves a thin sheaf of papers at me.

"Thanks," I say, taking them. I know I won't copy them because photocopying is 4p a sheet, but taking them means I have to give them back, which means an excuse to talk to her again.

"Want a chip?" she says, and she dips into her bag and pulls out a chip, then shoves it straight into my mouth. God, it's a turn-on being fed by her. And *God*, it tastes good. My stomach kind of seizes with wanting more. I chew it slowly, making massive eye contact with her, and she pouts up at me and says, "Hasn't he got great cheekbones?" Then she actually reaches out and strokes my face. "We should draw him."

I get an immediate groin-clench. Just from that contact. And Jenny giggles again, as though she knows.

"Any time, girls," I say, all smooth.

"Yeah? Life classes?"

In life classes, the models strip off. Right off. "You bet," I say. "Long as I get to do you the week after."

Portia laughs, and glides off on her way as though she's already wasted far too much time talking to a total no-hoper, and as she glides past a bin she dumps her bag of chips in. I'm behind her really fast and I pick up the bag of chips just as she's gliding out of the door and can't see me. The chip bag's nearly full and it wasn't up against anything manky, only a couple of Coke cans.

I stand there and stuff them in my mouth and tell myself I'm not really low and disgusting, picking things to eat out of litter bins. These are the chips of the woman I'm obsessed with, so it's like an erotic thing, a stalker's thing.

They taste *great*. How could she leave them? That's how she stays so fit and thin I suppose. I'm feeling quite chuffed with myself, thinking that was quite a hot little interchange, when some gossip I'd repressed surfaces to the front of my brain. This gossip is that Portia's got a new boyfriend. Only a few people have seen him but he looks about twenty-five and he's got a Golf GTI he picks her up from college in.

Shit. I finish the chips and mooch over to the counter to buy a cup of tea. Then I carry it over to an empty table by the window. The cafeteria's right by the college entrance, and from here I can look out on the concrete steps and the rubbish blowing about and the students walking in and out. I stare out and tell myself I'm a fool to even think about Portia, I'm a fool to starve so I can buy stamps to send off drawings to flashy companies who'll bin them soon as look at them, I'm a fool to—

"*LOOK*, you skiving little work-shy bastard, it's bad enough you skip my classes and never give anything in on time but when I'm reduced to tracking you down at the trough it really has gone beyond a BLOODY JOKE!"

Now read the rest!

HARD CASH *n.*
Coins and banknotes,
leading to freedom, potency,
style, possessions & sex

Then catch the sequel...
SHACKED UP *v.*
slang living together,
whether you like it or not

And watch out for the third book in the series...
Will Rich and Bonny stay together? Or is
Portia making a comeback?

If you enjoyed *SHOP DEAD*, you'll love:

FOOTLOOSE *adj.*
1. free to go or do
   as you please
2. eager to travel, restless

The ultimate beach novel!